Nikolai Leskov

The Lady Macbeth of the Mzinsk District

e-artnow 2020

Nikolai Leskov

The Lady Macbeth of the Mzinsk District

e-artnow, 2020
Contact: info@e-artnow.org

ISBN 978-80-273-0819-4

Contents

In our part of the country you sometimes meet people of whom, even many years after you have seen them, you are unable to think without a certain inward shudder. Such a character was the merchant's wife, Katerina Lvovna Izmaylova, who played the chief part in a terrible tragedy some time ago, and of whom the nobles of our district, adopting the light nickname somebody had given her, never spoke otherwise than as the Lady Macbeth of the Mzinsk District.

Katerina Lvovna was not really a beauty, but she was a woman of a very pleasing appearance. She was about twenty-four years of age; not very tall, but slim, with a neck that was like chiseled marble; she had soft round shoulders, firm breasts, a straight thin little nose, bright black eyes, a high white forehead, and black, almost blue black, hair. She came from Tuskar in the Kursk province and had married Izmaylov, a merchant of our place, not because she loved him or from any attraction towards him, but simply because he courted her, and she, being a poor girl, was not able to be too particular in making her choice of a husband. The firm of the Izmaylovs was one of the most considerable in our town; they dealt in wheaten flour, leased a large flour mill in the district, owned profitable fruit orchards not far from town, and in the town had a fine house. In a word, they were wealthy merchants. Their family was quite small. It consisted of her father-in-law, Boris Timofeich Izmaylov, a man of nearly eighty who had long been a widower; Zinovey Borisych Katerina Lvovna's husband, a man of over fifty; and Katerina Lvovna herself. Katerina Lvovna, who had now been married for five years, had no children. Zinovey Borisych had also no children from his first wife, with whom he had lived for twenty years before he became a widower and married Katerina Lvovna. He had thought and hoped that God would give him an heir by his second marriage to inherit his commercial name and fortune; but in this, too, he and Katerina Lvovna had no luck.

Not having children grieved Zinovey Borisych very much, and not only Zinovey Borisych, but also the old man Boris Timofeich, and it made even Katerina Lvovna herself very sad; first, because the immeasurable dullness of this secluded merchant's house, with its high fence and unchained watch-dogs, often made her feel so very melancholy that she almost went mad, and she would have been pleased, God knows how pleased, to have had a child to nurse; and also because she was tired of hearing reproaches: Why did she get married? What was the use of getting married? Why was she, a barren woman, bound by fate to a man? Just as if she had indeed committed a crime against her husband, against her father-in-law, and their whole race of honest merchants.

Notwithstanding all the wealth and plenty that surrounded her in her father-in-law's house, Katerina Lvovna's life was a very dull one. She seldom went to visit anyone, and even when she drove with her husband to any of his merchant friends, it was no pleasure. The people were all strict: they watched how she sat down, how she walked across the room, how she got up. Now Katerina Lvovna had a passionate nature, and having been brought up in poverty she was accustomed to simplicity and freedom: running with pails to the river for water, bathing under the pier in a shift, or scattering sun-flower seeds over the gate on to the head of any young fellow who might be passing by. Here all was different. Her father-in-law and her husband got up early, drank tea at six o'clock, and then went out to their business, and she stayed behind, to roam about the house from one room to another. Everywhere it was clean, everywhere it was quiet and empty; the lamps glimmered before the icons; but nowhere in the house could you hear the sound of life or a human voice.

Katerina Lvovna would wander about the empty rooms, and begin to yawn because she was dull. Then mounting the stairs to their conjugal chamber, which was in a high, small attic, she would sit down at the window and look at the men weighing hemp or filling sacks with flour-she would yawn again-she was glad to feel sleepy-she would then take a nap for an hour or two, and when she awoke-there was the same dullness, the Russian dullness, the dullness of a merchant's house, which they say makes it quite a pleasure to strangle oneself. Katerina

Lvovna did not like reading and even had she liked it there were no books in the house except the Kiev Lives of the Fathers.

This was the dull life Katerina Lvovna had lived in the house of her rich father-in-law all the five years of her married life with her indifferent husband; but nobody, as usual, took the slightest notice of her loneliness.

In the spring of the sixth year of Katerina Lvovna's married life the dam of the Izmaylov's mill burst. Just at that time, as if on purpose, much work had been brought to the mill, and the damages were very extensive. The water had washed away the lower beams of the mill-race, and it had been impossible to stop it in a hurry. Zinovey Borisych had collected workmen from the whole district at the mill, and himself remained there permanently. The town business was carried on by the old man, and Katerina Lvovna languished at home quite alone for days on end. At first she was even duller without her husband, but after a time it seemed to her better so; she was freer when alone. Her heart had never been very greatly drawn towards him, and without him at any rate there was one less to order her about.

One day Katerina Lvovna was sitting at the small window of her attic; she yawned thinking of nothing in particular, and at last became ashamed of yawning. The weather was beautiful-warm, light, gay-and through the green wooden palings of the garden one could see the playful birds in the trees fluttering about from branch to branch.

"I wonder why I am yawning so," thought Katerina Lvovna. "Well, I might get up and walk about the yard, or go into the garden."

Katerina Lvovna threw an old cloth jacket over her shoulders and went out.

Out of doors it was light, and you could take deep long breaths, and in the shed near the warehouse such gay laughter was heard.

"Why are you so merry?" said Katerina Lvovna to her father-in-law's clerk.

"Little Mother, Katerina Lvovna, it's because they are weighing a live pig," answered the old clerk.

"What! A pig?"

"It is that pig Aksinia, who gave birth to a son, Vassili, and never invited us to the christening," answered a merry, bold young fellow. He had an impudent good-looking face, framed in curly coal-black locks, and a little beard that was only just beginning to grow.

At that moment the fat red face of the cook Aksinia looked out of the flour vat which was hanging to the beam of the weighing machine.

"You devils, you smooth faced imps!" the cook swore, trying to catch hold of the iron beam and get out of the swaying vat.

"She weighs eight pouds before dinner, but when she has eaten a pile of hay there wont be enough weights!" the good-looking young fellow continued, to explain, and turning the vat over he threw the cook out on some sacks that were heaped up in a corner.

The woman abusing them laughingly began to tidy herself.

"Well, and how much would I weigh?" said Katerina Lvovna jokingly, and taking hold of the rope got on to the weighing machine.

"Three pouds and seven pounds," answered the same good-looking Sergei, throwing the weights on to the machine. "Wonderful."

"What are you wondering at?"

"That you weigh three pouds, Katerina Lvovna. One would have to carry you all day long in one's arms, I reckon, before getting exhausted-it would only be a pleasure."

"What, am I not like other people, eh? If you carried me, never fear, you would get just as tired," answered Katerina Lvovna, blushing slightly. She was unused to such words, and she suddenly felt a desire to chatter and say all sorts of gay, jolly things.

"Certainly not! Good Lord! I would carry you to Arabia the Blessed," answered Sergei to her remark.

"Young man, you don't argue correctly," said the peasant who was filling the sacks. "What is of weight in us? Is it our body that weighs? Our body, my good fellow, counts for nothing on the scales: it's our strength, our strength, that weighs-not our body!"

"Yes, when I was a girl, I was terribly strong," said Katerina Lvovna, who was unable to restrain herself. "Not every man could get the better of me."

"Well, then, if that is so, give me your little hand," said the handsome young fellow.

Katerina Lvovna became confused, but held out her hand.

"Oh, let go of my ring, it hurts!" cried Katerina Lvovna, when Sergei squeezed her hand in his; and with her free hand she gave him a blow on the chest.

The young fellow released the mistress's hand and her blow made him stagger two paces backwards.

"So that's how you can judge a woman," said the surprised peasant.

"No, allow me to try to wrestle with you?" said Sergei, throwing back his curls.

"Very well, try," answered Katerina Lvovna gaily, and she lifted up her elbows.

Sergei put his arms round the young mistress, and pressed her firm breasts to his red shirt. Katerina Lvovna could only make a slight movement of her shoulders, and Sergei lifted her from the floor, held her up in the air, pressed her to himself, and then gently set her down on the overturned vat.

Katerina Lvovna had no time even to attempt to make use of her boasted strength. She looked very red as she sat on the measure and arranged the jacket on her shoulders, and then quietly went out of the warehouse; while Sergei coughed vigorously and shouted:

"Now then, you blockheads! Don't stand and gape. Fill the sacks and give level measure; strict measure is our gain." Just as if he were paying no heed to what had just occurred.

"He's always after the girls, that damned Serezhka," said the cook Aksinia, as she waddled after Katerina Lvovna. "The rascal is attractive in every way-fine body, fine face, good looks. He will coax and flatter any woman you like-and then lead her to sin. He is a fickle scoundrel too-as fickle as you make 'em!"

"And you, Aksinia, what about you?" said the young mistress walking in front. "Is your boy still alive?"

"He's alive, little mother, he's alive. Why shouldn't he be? They always live where they're not wanted."

"Whose is he?"

"Eh, who's to know? One lives in a crowd-one walks about with many."

"Has that young fellow been long with us?"

"Which young fellow? Do you mean Sergei?"

"Yes."

"About a month. He served before at Konchonov's. The master kicked him out." Aksinia lowered her voice and continued: "They say he had a love affair with the mistress there. The cursed young scamp! See how bold he is!"

III

A warm milky twilight hung over the town. Zinovey Borisych had not yet returned from the work at the dam. The father-in-law Boris Timofeich was not at home either; he had gone to the celebration of an old friend's name-day, and had said he would not be home for supper. Katerina Lvovna, having nothing to do, had retired early to her room, and opening the little window of her attic, sat leaning against the window-post, cracking sunflower seeds. The servants had finished their supper in the kitchen and had gone to bed, some in the barn, some in the warehouse, and others in the high sweet-scented hay loft. Sergei was the last to leave the kitchen. He walked about the yard, unchained the watch-dogs, and passed whistling under Katerina Lvovna's window. He looked up at her and bowed low.

"How do you do?" Katerina Lvovna said to him quietly from her attic, and the yard became silent as if it were a desert.

"Madam!" said somebody, five minutes later at Katerina Lvovna's locked door.

"Who's there?" asked Katerina Lvovna, frightened.

"Don't be afraid! It's I, Sergei," answered the clerk.

"Sergei? What do you want?"

"I have a little business with you, Katerina Lvovna; I want to ask your gracious self about a small matter. Allow me to come in for a moment."

Katerina Lvovna turned the key and let Sergei in.

"What do you want?" she said, going to the window.

"I have come to you, Katerina Lvovna, to ask if you have some book you could give me to read. It helps to drive away boredom."

"No, Sergei, I have no books. I do not read them," answered Katerina Lvovna.

"It's so dull!" Sergei complained.

"Why should you feel dull?"

"Good gracious, how can I help feeling dull? I'm a young man; we live here like in a monastery, and the only future to be seen is that we shall go on stagnating in this solitude till we are under the coffin-lid. It makes one sometimes despair."

"Why don't you get married?"

"It's easy, madam, to say get married. Whom can one marry here? I'm only an unimportant man. A master's daughter won't marry me, and owing to poverty, as you yourself know, Katerina Lvovna, I have not much education. How could such a girl know anything about real love? Surely you have noticed how rich merchants understand it. Now you, one may say, would be a comfort to any man who has any feelings, but they keep you in a cage like a canary-bird."

"Yes, I am dull," exclaimed Katerina Lvovna involuntarily.

"How can one help being dull, madam, in such a life? Even if you had another, as others have, it would be impossible to see him."

"Why, what do you mean? It's not that at all. If only I had had a child, I think I should be merry with it."

"Yes, but allow me to say madam, even a child comes from somewhere and not out of the clouds. Do you think, that now having lived so many years with masters, and having seen the sort of life the women have among merchants, we also don't understand? The song says: 'Without a dear friend, sadness and grief possess thee.' And this sadness, I must inform you, Katerina Lvovna, has made my heart feel so tender, that I could take a steel knife to cut it out of my breast and throw it at your little feet. It would be easier, a hundred times easier for me then . . . ."

Sergei's voice shook.

"Why are you telling me about your heart? I have nothing to do with it. Go away . . . ."

"No, allow me, madam," said Sergei, trembling all over and taking a step towards Katerina Lvovna. "I know, I see, I feel and understand quite well that your lot is no better than mine in this world; but now," said he, drawing a long breath, "now at this moment, all this is in your hands, and in your power."

"What do you mean? —Why have you come to me? —I shall throw myself out of the window," said Katerina Lvovna, feeling herself under the intolerable power of an indescribable terror, and she caught hold of the window sill.

"My life! My incomparable one, why should you throw yourself out of the window?" whispered Sergei boldly, and tearing the young mistress away from the window he pressed her in a close embrace.

"Oh, oh, let me go," Katerina Lvovna sighed gently, becoming weak under Sergei's hot kisses, and she pressed, contrary to her own wish, closer to his strong body.

Sergei lifted the mistress up in his arms like a child and carried her to a dark corner.

A silence fell upon the room, which was only broken by the soft regular ticking of a watch, belonging to Katerina Lvovna's husband, which hung over the head of the bed; but this did not disturb them.

"Go," said Katerina Lvovna half an hour later, without looking at Sergei, as she arranged her disordered hair before a small mirror.

"Why should I go away from here now," answered Sergei in a joyful voice.

"My father-in-law will lock the door."

"Eh, my dear, my dear! What sort of people have you known, that you think the only road to a woman is through a door? To come to you, or to go from you there are doors everywhere for me," said the young fellow, pointing to the columns that supported the gallery.

IV

For more than a week Zinovey Borisych did not return, and the whole time his wife spent every night, till the white dawn, with Sergei.

In those nights much happened in Zinovey Borisych's bedroom: wine from the father-in-law's cellar was drunk; dainty sweetmeats eaten; many kisses taken from the mistress's sugared lips, and black locks toyed with on the soft pillows. But not every road is smooth: some have ruts.

Boris Timofeich could not sleep. The old man in his coloured print shirt wandered about the quiet house; he went up to one window, went up to another, looked out, and saw Sergei in a red shirt quietly sliding down the column from his daughter-in-law's window. "What's this?"

Boris Timofeich hurried out and caught the young fellow by the leg. Sergei turned round wanting to give him a box on the ear, with his whole strength, but stopped, remembering the noise it would make.

"Tell me where you have been, you young thief?" said Boris Timofeich.

"Wherever it was, Boris Timofeich," said Sergei, "I am no longer there."

"Have you spent the night with my daughter-in-law?"

"Well, as to that, master, I know where I have passed the night; but, Boris Timofeich, listen to my words; what is done can't be undone, father. Don't disgrace your merchant's house by taking extreme measures. Tell me what you require of me now? What amends do you want?"

"You asp, I want to give you five hundred lashes," answered Boris Timofeich.

"As you will-it's my fault," agreed the young man. "Tell me where to go; do as you please-you may drink my blood."

Boris Timofeich took Sergei to his little stone store-room, and lashed him with his whip until he had no more strength. Sergei did not utter a groan, but instead he chewed half his shirt sleeve away.

Boris Timofeich left Sergei in the store-room for the bruises on his back to heal, gave him an earthen jug of water, locked the door with a great padlock, and sent for his son.

In Russia even now you can't drive fast over by-ways, and Katerina Lvovna could not live a single hour without Sergei. Her awakened nature had suddenly developed to its full breadth, and she had become so resolute that it was impossible to restrain her. She found out where Sergei was, talked with him through the iron door, and hurried away to look for the keys. "Daddy, let Sergei out," said she coming to her father-in-law.

The old man turned green. He had never expected such brazen-faced insolence from his erring daughter-in-law, who till then had always been obedient

"What do you mean, you ——" and he began to revile Katerina Lvovna.

"Let him out," said she. "I can answer with a clear conscience that as yet nothing wrong has passed between us."

"No wrong has happened," said he, "and there he is grinding his teeth. What did you do with him at night there? Did you restuff your husband's pillows?"

But she only repeated the same words: "Let him out, let him out."

"If that is so," said Boris Timofeich, "this is what you shall have for reward: Your husband shall come, and we will take you, you honest wife, to the stable, and whip you with our own hands, and to-morrow that rascal shall be sent to prison."

This is what Boris Timofeich decided. His decision, however, was not carried out.

V

Boris Timofeich ate mushrooms with gruel for supper; he got a heart-burn from it. Then suddenly he had pains in the pit of the stomach, terrible vomitings began and he died before morning. He died just like the rats in his granary, for which Katerina Lvovna had always prepared, with her own hands, a certain kind of food made of a dangerous white powder that had been entrusted to her.

Katerina Lvovna let Sergei out of the old man's store-room and brazenly laid him publicly in her husband's bed to recover from the blows that her father-in-law had inflicted on him. Her father-in-law was buried according to the rites of the Christian Church. Nobody was surprised at this strange occurrence. Boris Timofeich was dead, and had died after eating mushrooms, as many die after eating them. Boris Timofeich was buried hurriedly without waiting for his son to arrive; it was very hot weather, and the messenger who had been sent to him did not find Zinovey Borisych at the mill. He had heard of a forest that was for sale a hundred versts farther off, and had gone there to inspect it, without telling anybody which road he had taken.

Having settled this business Katerina Lvovna became quite changed. She had never been one of your timid women, but now you could not guess what she would do next. She went about like an empress, gave orders to everybody, and did not let Sergei leave her for a moment. The people in the yard were surprised at this; but Katerina Lvovna managed to reach all of them with her bountiful hand, and their surprise suddenly ceased. They understood that the mistress had some sort of business with Sergei —"that's all. It's her affair-she will have to answer for it."

By this time Sergei had recovered; he grew straight again and became again the same smart young fellow, like a live falcon at Katerina Lvovna's side, and their life of love making recommenced! But it was not only for them that time passed; the injured husband was hastening home after his long absence.

VI

In the afternoon the heat was baking and the nimble flies were unbearably irritating.

Katerina Lvovna had closed the shutters of the bedroom window, hung a woollen shawl across it, and had laid herself down with Sergei to rest on the merchant's high bed. Katerina Lvovna was scarcely asleep, but oppressed by the heat, her face was wet with perspiration and her breath came hot and heavy. She felt it was time to wake up, that it was time to go into the garden to have tea, but she could not move. At last the cook knocked at the door and announced that the samovar was getting cold under the apple tree. Katerina Lvovna with scarcely opened eyes began to caress the cat. The cat squeezed itself in between Sergei and her. It was such a fine grey cat, large and fat, with whiskers like a tax-collector's. Katerina Lvovna began to stroke his thick fur. He stretched out his head to her, thrust his blunt nose coaxingly against her firm breasts and began to sing a soft song, as if he were telling her of love. "I wonder why this cat has come here?" thought Katerina Lvovna. "I put some cream on the window sill; I am sure the rascal has lapped it up. I must turn him out," she decided and wanted to seize hold of him and put him out of the room, but he seemed to slip away between her fingers like a mist. "How has this cat come here?" Katerina Lvovna thought in her dream. "We have never had a cat in our bedroom and now see what a fine one has got in." She again tried to catch the cat, but again it was not there. "What can it be? I wonder if it is a cat at all?" thought Katerina Lvovna. A panic seized her and drove both her dream and her sleep quite away. Katerina Lvovna looked round the room; there was no cat anywhere, only handsome Sergei lying there and with his strong hand pressing her breast to his hot face.

Katerina Lvovna rose, sat down on the bed, kissed and caressed Sergei many times, arranged the disordered feather bed, and went into the garden to drink tea. The sun was already low, and a beautiful, enchanting evening was settling down on the hot earth.

"I have slept too long," said Katerina Lvovna to Aksinia as she sat down on a carpet under the flowering apple tree to drink tea. "What does this mean, Aksinia?" she asked the cook as she wiped a saucer with the tea-cloth.

"What, little mother?"

"It was not like a dream, but I saw quite clearly a cat creep up to me."

"Really!"

"It's quite true a cat crept up to me," and Katerina Lvovna related how the cat had crept up to her.

"Why did you fondle it?"

"That's just it. I don't know why I did."

"Wonderful, certainly!" exclaimed the cook.

"I can't help being astonished."

"It certainly seems as if somebody will come to you, don't you think, or as if something will happen?"

"At first I dreamed of the moon, and then of this cat," continued Katerina Lvovna.

"The moon, that means a baby."

Katerina Lvovna blushed.

"Should I not send Sergei to your honour?" said Aksinia trying to obtain confidences.

"Well, why not!" answered Katerina Lvovna, "that's a good idea. Go and send him to me, I will treat him to tea here."

"Well, well, just as I thought. I will send him," and Aksinia waddled off like a duck towards the garden gate.

Katerina Lvovna also told Sergei about the cat.

"Only dreams," answered Sergei.

"Why have these dreams never been before?"

"Many things have not been before. Formerly I could only look at you with my eyes and pine for you, and now behold! Your whole white body is mine."

Sergei caught Katerina Lvovna in his arms, swung her round in the air, and playfully threw her down on the thick carpet.

"Oh, I am quite giddy!" said Katerina Lvovna. "Serezha, come here and sit down next to me," she called to him tenderly as she stretched herself out luxuriously.

The young fellow bent down, got under the low branches of the apple tree, which were covered with white blossoms, and seated himself on the carpet at Katerina Lvovna's feet.

"So you pined for me, Serezha!"

"How could I not pine for you?"

"How did you pine for me? Tell me all about it."

"How can one explain it? Is it possible to explain how one pines away? I was melancholy!"

"Serezha, why did I not feel that you were dying for me? They say that can be felt."

Sergei remained silent.

"Why did you sing songs if you were longing for me? Why? I heard you, believe me, singing under the shed." Katerina Lvovna continued to question, fondling him all the time.

"What if I did sing songs? The gnats sing their whole life, but not for joy," answered Sergei dryly.

There was a pause. Sergei's confessions filled Katerina Lvovna with great delight.

She wanted to talk, but Sergei frowned and was silent.

"Look, Sergei, what a paradise, a paradise," cried Katerina Lvovna gazing up through the thick branches of the flowering apple tree, into the blue sky where the full moon hung serenely.

The moonlight streaming through the leaves and flowers of the apple tree fell in the strangest bright spots on Katerina Lvovna's face and figure, as she lay on her back beneath it. The air was still; only a light warm breeze gently moved the sleepy leaves and brought with it the faint scent of flowering herbs and trees. It was difficult to breathe and one felt an inclination to laziness, indulgence, and dark desires.

Katerina Lvovna not receiving an answer was again silent, and continued to gaze at the sky through the pale pink blossoms of the apple tree. Sergei remained silent too, but he was not interested in the sky; clasping his knees with both arms he sat concentrating his gaze on his boots.

A golden night! Stillness, light, aroma and beneficent, vivifying warmth. On the other side of the garden, in the distance beyond the ravine, someone struck up a loud song; near the fence in a thicket of bird-cherries a nightingale poured forth its shrill song; in a cage on a high pole a sleepy quail jumped about; the fat horse breathed heavily behind the stable wall; and on the other side of the garden fence a pack of gay dogs ran noiselessly across the common and disappeared in the strange, formless, black shade of the old, half-ruined salt-warehouses.

Katerina Lvovna leaned on her elbow and looked at the high grass of the garden; the grass seemed to be playing with the moonbeams, that fell in small flickers on the leaves and blossoms of the trees.

All was gilded by these capricious bright spots that twinkled and trembled everywhere like fiery butterflies, as if the grass under the trees had been caught in a net of moonbeams and moved from side to side.

"Ah, Serezhechka, how beautiful," cried Katerina Lvovna, looking round.

Sergei looked round with indifference.

"Serezha, why are you so joyless? Are you already tired of my love?"

"Don't talk nonsense," answered Sergei shortly, and bending down kissed Katerina Lvovna lazily.

"You're fickle, Serezha," said Katerina Lvovna, feeling jealous. "You're not constant."

"I won't accept these words as applying to me," said Sergei quietly.

"Why do you kiss me in that way?"

Sergei became quite silent.

"It is only husbands and wives" continued Katerina Lvovna playing with his curls, "who take the dust off each others lips in that way. Kiss me now so that the young blossoms of the apple tree above us shall fall to the earth."

"In this way, in this way," whispered Katerina Lvovna embracing her lover and kissing him with passionate abandonment.

"Listen, Serezha to what I tell you," began Katerina Lvovna a little later, "why is it that everybody with one voice says that you are a deceiver?"

"Who cares to tell lies about me?"

"Well, people say so."

"Perhaps, at some time, I may have been false to those who were quite unworthy."

"And pray why did you have anything to do with the unworthy, you fool? It is stupid to make love to the worthless."

"It's all very well to talk! Is this a matter one can reason about? Temptation leads you astray. You have acted towards a woman quite simply, without regard to any of those commandments, and she hangs herself on your neck. And there you have love."

"Listen, Serezha, I don't know what others there may have been, and don't want to know about them, but how you managed to persuade me, how you seduced me to our present love; you yourself know; how much was my desire, how much your cunning; but if you betray me for another, Serezha; if you leave me for any other, forgive me, sweetheart, for telling you, I will not part from you alive."

Sergei shuddered.

"But, Katerina Lvovna, you are my bright light," he began. "You can see for yourself how our affair stands. You have just remarked that I am melancholy to-day, and you don't reflect how I can be otherwise. Perhaps my whole heart is drenched with frozen blood."

"Tell me, Serezha, tell me your grief."

"What can I tell you? Here first of all, God help me, your husband will return; then, you, Sergei Filipych, must go away; go along to the back yard, to the musicians, and you can look out of the barn and see how the little candles burn in Katerina Lvovna's bedroom; how she shakes up her feather-bed, and how she is getting ready to sleep with her lawful husband, Zinovey Borisych."

"That will never be," said Katerina Lvovna gaily, and she waved her arms.

"What do you mean—'never be'? As I understand it, it can't be otherwise. I, too, Katerina Lvovna, have a heart and can see my own torments."

"That's enough, why keep on talking about it?"

It pleased Katerina Lvovna to see this expression of jealousy in Sergei, and she laughed and began to kiss him again.

"But I repeat," continued Sergei, quietly drawing his head away from Katerina Lvovna's arms that were bare to the shoulders, "I must own too that my miserable position causes me to reflect, not once but ten times, how it will all end. If I were, so to speak, your equal; if I were a gentleman, or a merchant, I would never part from you, Katerina Lvovna, in my whole life; but you can judge for yourself what sort of a man I am compared to you. When I see you now taken by your little white hand and led into the bedchamber, I must bear it all in my heart; and can even become in my own eyes a despised man for the rest of my life, Katerina Lvovna! I am not like the others who don't mind anything if they can only get pleasure from a woman. I feel what love is, and how like a black snake it is sucking my heart. . . ."

"Why are you telling me all this?" interrupted Katerina Lvovna.

She was sorry for Sergei.

"Katerina Lvovna, I must talk about it? How can I help talking about it? Supposing everything is explained and described to him; supposing, not only at some distant time, but even tomorrow, Sergei will no longer be here in flesh or in spirit?"

"No, no, don't talk about it, Serezha. This can never be. I can never exist without you," Katerina Lvovna said trying to comfort him with more of the same caresses. "If things come to that point, that either he or I cannot live-you will still be with me."

"This can never be, Katerina Lvovna," answered Seregi sadly, and he shook his head gloomily. "My life is miserable because of this love. If I loved someone no better than myself, I would be satisfied. How can I have your love for ever? Would it be an honour for you-to be my sweetheart? I want to become your husband in the holy eternal Church, and though I would always count myself unworthy of you, still I could show the whole world what the respect of my wife had made me worthy of . . . ."

Katerina Lvovna was dazed by Sergei's words, by his jealousy, by his desire to marry her —a desire that is pleasing to every woman, no matter how intimate her relations have been with the man before marriage. Katerina Lvovna was ready to go through fire and water, to prison, or to the cross for Sergei. He had succeeded in making her so much in love with him, that there was no limit to her devotion. Her happiness made her mad, her blood boiled, and she could listen to nothing else. With a rapid motion she covered Sergei's mouth with the palm of her hand, and pressing his head to her breast she began to speak.

"Yes, I know how I can make you a merchant, and how I can live with you in quite the proper way. Only, you must not make me sad for nothing before our affairs are settled."

And again there were kisses and endearments.

The old clerk, who was sleeping in the barn, heard in the stillness of the night through his sound sleep whispers and low laughter, as if some roguish children were plotting together how they could better deride decrepit old age; or again, loud and gay laughter as if some one was tickling the water nymph of the lake. But it was only Katerina Lvovna who was gambolling and rolling about in the moonlight and who wantoned and played on the soft carpet with her husband's young clerk. The blossoming apple trees shed their young petals over them, till at last they also ceased to fall. By that time the short summer night was passing away; the moon hid behind the steep roof of the granary and looked askance on the earth as it became dimmer and dimmer. From the roof of the kitchen a piercing cats' duet resounded, and then after angry spittings and splutters, two or three dishevelled cats rushed down a pile of boards that were propped up against the roof.

"Let's go to bed," said Katerina Lvovna, rising slowly, as if exhausted, from the carpet, and just as she had been lying there, in her shift and white petticoats, she went across the quiet, the deadly quiet, merchant's yard, while Sergei followed her carrying the carpet and her blouse, which she had thrown off in her frolics.

VII

Katerina Lvovna had scarcely had time to blow out her candle and to lie down on the soft feather-bed quite undressed, before sleep overpowered her. She was so tired after playing and diverting herself that she slept soundly; even her legs and arms slept; but again, as if in a dream, she heard the door open, and again the cat jumped with great agility on to the bed.

"Really it is a punishment to have this cat always here," reflected Katerina Lvovna wearily. "I locked the door on purpose with my own hands, the window is shut too and here he is again. I will turn him out directly," said Katerina Lvovna, trying to get up, but her sleepy arms and legs would not obey her, and the cat crept over her and mewed so strangely, that it sounded again as if it was uttering human speech. A cold shiver passed over Katerina Lvovna's whole body.

"No," thought she, "there is nothing else to be done; to-morrow I must certainly get some consecrated water and sprinkle the bed with it, because this is a most mysterious cat that is always coming to me."

But the cat purred and mewed close to her ear, stuck its muzzle into it, and said:

"What sort of a cat am I? Why should I be a cat? You, Katerina Lvovna, very wisely think that I am not a cat. I am really the well-known merchant Boris Timofeich. I am only feeling bad now, because all my inside has been split owing to the treat my daughter-in-law gave me. That is why I mew; I have grown small in size, and appear like a cat to those who little think who I really am. How are you, Katerina Lvovna, and what sort of a life are you living with us? How faithfully do you keep your vow? I have come from the churchyard on purpose to see how you and Sergei Filipych are warming your husband's bed. It's all dark, you can play about, I see nothing. Don't be afraid of me. You see your treat has made my eyes rot away. Look at my eyes, my little friend, don't be afraid."

Katerina Lvovna glanced at him, and shrieked at the top of her voice. Between her and Sergei the cat was lying and its head was the full-sized head of Boris Timofeich, just as he had been as a corpse, only instead of eyes fiery circles whirled round and round in every direction.

Sergei awoke and comforted Katerina Lvovna, and again fell asleep; but for her sleep had departed; and it was well, too, that it had.

She lay with open eyes, when suddenly she seemed to hear a sound as if someone had climbed over the gate and was in the yard. The dogs began to bark, but soon ceased-they were probably being fondled. Another minute passed and she heard the key turn in the iron lock, and the door open. "Either I am dreaming or my Zinovey Borisych has returned, because the door has been opened with his latch-key," thought Katerina Lvovna and hastily nudged Sergei.

"Listen, Serezha," said she raising herself on her elbow and listening attentively.

Some one was really coming up the stairs, carefully placing his feet on the steps and approaching the locked door of the bedroom.

Katerina Lvovna hurriedly sprang out of bed in only her nightdress and opened the window. At the same moment Sergei bare-footed jumped out into the gallery, and his legs clasped the column by which he had many times descended from the mistress's bedroom.

"No, don't, don't. Lie down here, don't go far," whispered Katerina Lvovna, throwing his boots and clothes to him out of the window, and then slipped under the bed-clothes again and waited.

Sergei obeyed Katerina Lvovna; he did not slide down the column but hid under a shelf in the gallery.

Meanwhile Katerina Lvovna heard her husband come to the door and listen, holding his breath. She could even hear the rapid beating of his jealous heart; but she had no sorrow for him, only an evil laugh seized her.

"What's done can't be undone," she thought smiling and breathing like an innocent child.

This lasted for about ten minutes, but at last Zinovey Borisych got tired of standing on the other side of the door listening to his wife's breathing in her sleep, so he knocked.

"Who is there?" called Katerina Lvovna after a little time, feigning a sleepy voice.

"A friend," answered Zinovey Borisych.

"Is it you, Zinovey Borisych?"

"Of course it's I—as if you don't hear?"

Katerina Lvovna jumped out of bed, and in her shift just as she was, let her husband in and again dived into the warm bed.

"It somehow gets cold before dawn," said she wrapping herself up in the quilt.

Zinovey Borisych came in, looked round, said a prayer, lit a candle, and again looked round.

"How are you getting on?" he asked his wife.

"All right," answered Katerina Lvovna, and sitting up she began putting on a loose cotton blouse.

"I'm sure you'd like me to put on the samovar?" she asked.

"Oh, don't bother; call Aksinia, and let her do it."

Katerina Lvovna slipped her feet into her shoes and ran out of the room. It was more than half an hour before the returned. During that time she had blown the charcoal into a glow in the samovar and had quickly fluttered up to Sergei in the gallery.

"Remain here," she whispered.

"How long?" asked Sergei also in a whisper.

"Oh, how stupid you are! Stay here, till I call you."

And Katerina Lvovna hid him again in the same place.

From where he was in the gallery Sergei could hear everything that happened in the bedroom. He heard the door slam when Katerina Lvovna again went back to her husband. He could hear every word that was said.

"What have you been doing all this time," Zinovey Boirsych asked his wife.

"I have been getting the samovar to boil," she answered quietly.

There was a pause. Sergei could hear Zinovey Borisych hang his coat on the pegs. Then he washed, snorting and splashing the water about; he asked for a towel and they again began to talk.

"Well, how did you come to bury father?" inquired her husband.

"He just died and was buried," answered his wife.

"What a strange thing it was!"

"God only knows," answered Katerina Lvovna, and began to rattle the cups.

Zinovey Borisych walked about the room gloomily.

"Well, and you? How have you passed your time?" Zinovey Borisych asked his wife.

"Our pleasures are known to everybody. We don't go to balls, nor to theatres either."

"It appears you are not very pleased to see your husband," observed Zinovey Borisych giving her a sudden glance.

"We are not such young things, you and I, that we should go out of our senses when we meet. How am I to show my delight? Here am I, fussing and running about to please you."

Katerina Lvovna again went out of the room to fetch the samovar, and again had time to run up to Sergei, nudge him, and whisper:

"Don't doze, Sergei, be ready."

Sergei could not understand to what all this was to lead; but he waited ready to be called.

When Katerina Lvovna returned to the room Zinovey Borisych was kneeling on the bed, hanging his silver watch and beadwork chain on the wall at the head of the bed.

"Katerina Lvovna, why have you made the bed for two when you were alone?" He asked his wife suddenly as if surprised.

"I was always expecting you," Katerina Lvovna answered calmly, looking at him.

"Even for that we must thank you humbly. But how did this thing happen to be lying on the feather-bed?"

Zinovey Borisych lifted Sergei's narrow woollen girdle from the sheet and held it up by the end before his wife's eyes.

Katerina Lvovna answered without hesitation:

"I found it in the garden, and tied my petticoat up with it."

"Yes!" said Zinovey Borisych with special emphasis, "we have also heard something about your petticoats."

"What have you heard about them?"

"About all the fine things you have done."

"I have done no fine things."

"Well, we shall soon find that out; we shall find out everything," answered Zinovey Borisych, pushing his empty cup towards his wife.

Katerina Lvovna remained silent.

"We shall bring all your actions to the light, Katerina Lvovna," said Zinovey Borisych after a long pause, frowning at her.

"Your Katerina Lvovna is not easily frightened; she is not much afraid of that," she answered.

"What's all this?" cried Zinovey Borisych raising his voice.

"Nothing-it's all over," answered his wife.

"Well-you just take care, you're getting too talkative!"

"Why can't I talk?" exclaimed Katerina Lvovna.

"You ought to have been more cautious."

"I have nothing to be cautious about. Much I care for what long-tongued vipers may have told you. Am I to put up with all sorts of abuse? That's something new."

"There are no long tongues; but they know all about your amours."

"About which of my amours?" cried Katerina Lvovna, getting angry in earnest.

"I know very well which."

"If you know, what then? You'd better be a little more explicit!"

Zinovey Borisych was silent and again pushed his cup towards her.

"Apparently you have nothing to say," cried Katerina Lvovna with contempt angrily throwing a tea spoon on her husband's saucer. "Well, can't you say who has been accused? Who in your eyes is my lover?"

"You will hear; no need to hurry so."

"Is it about Sergei, perhaps, that they have been lying to you?"

"We shall find out, we shall find out, Katerina Lvovna; nobody can take away our authority over you, and nobody has a right to do so . . . . You yourself will tell us. . . ."

"Oh, I can't bear it," cried Katerina Lvovna, grinding her teeth, and getting as white as a sheet she suddenly ran out of the room.

"Well, there he is," said she a few seconds later re-entering the room and leading Sergei by the sleeve. "Now you can question him and me too about what you know. Perhaps you will hear even more than you want to."

Zinovey Borisych became confused. Looking from Sergei, who stood near the door, to his wife, who had calmly sat down on the edge of the bed and folded her arms, he could not understand where all this was leading.

"What are you doing, you snake?" He was scarcely able to utter and did not rise from his arm-chair.

"Question us about what you pretend to know so well," Katerina Lvovna answered audaciously. "You thought to frighten me with your power," continued she significantly flashing her eyes on him; "that will never happen; but what I know I would do to you, perhaps even before your threats, that I will do."

"What does this mean? Get out!" Zinovey Borisych shouted at Sergei.

"Make him," said Katerina Lvovna with a sneer.

She went quietly to the door, locked it, and putting the key in her pocket lolled again on the bed.

"Now then Serezhenka come, come here, my darling," she said, coaxing the clerk towards her.

Sergei shook his curls and boldly sat down near the mistress.

"Good Lord! My God! what is this? What are you doing, you savages," cried Zinovey Borisych getting livid and rising from his chair.

"What? Don't you like it? See here, see here; my bright-eyed falcon, isn't he a beauty?"

Katerina Lvovna laughed and kissed Sergei passionately before her husband's eyes.

At that moment she received a deafening blow on her cheek, and Zinovey Borisych hurried to the open window.

"Oh, so that's it! Well, my dear friend, thank you. I was only waiting for this," cried Katerina Lvovna. "Now one can see it will be neither your way nor my way."

With a sharp movement she threw Sergei from her and pounced on her husband from behind, and before Zinovey Borisych had time to reach the window, she had seized his throat with her thin fingers, and had thrown him on the floor like a sheaf of damp hemp.

Falling heavily Zinovey Borisych struck the back of his head against the floor with such force that he was quite dazed. He had not expected such a quick ending. This first act of violence that his wife had used against him proved to him that she was prepared for anything if she could only free herself from him, and that his present position was one of great danger. Zinovey Borisych realized this in an instant, at the moment of his fall, and did not cry out, knowing that his voice could not reach anybody's ears and might only hasten the end. He looked round in silence, and with an expression of wrath, reproach and suffering, his eyes rested on his wife, whose thin fingers were tightly squeezing his throat.

Zinovey Borisych did not defend himself; his arms, with tightly clenched fists, lay stretched out jerking spasmodically; one of them was quite free; the other Katerina Lvovna pressed to the floor with her knee.

"Hold him," she whispered to Sergei in an indifferent voice and again turned to her husband.

Sergei sat down on the master, pressing his two arms down with his knees, and tried to seize him by the throat under Katerina Lvovna's hands, but at the same moment he uttered a cry of despair. The sight of the man who had wronged him, and the desire for bloody revenge aroused in Zinovey Borisych all his remaining strength, and with a violent effort he was able to free his imprisoned arms from the weight of Sergei's knees, and seizing hold of Sergei's black locks he bit at his throat like a wild beast. But it was not for long; Zinovey Borisych groaned heavily and his head fell back.

Katerina Lvovna, pale and hardly breathing, stood over her husband and lover; in her right hand she had a heavy metal candlestick, which she was holding by the top with the heavy part downwards. A thin stream of red blood trickled down Zinovey Borisych's temple and cheek.

"A priest . . ." Zinovey Borisych groaned hoarsely, and with loathing drew his head away as far as he could from Sergei, who was still sitting on him, ". . . to confess," he uttered still less distinctly, shivering and looking sideways at the hot blood that was thickening under his hair.

"You're good enough without that," murmured Katerina Lvovna.

"Enough trifling with him," she said to Sergei, "catch hold of his throat properly."

Zinovey Borisych gasped.

Katerina Lvovna stooped down and pressing her own hands over Sergei's, that were tightly clasped round her husband's throat, put her ear to his breast. After five quiet minutes she got up and said: "Enough; that will do for him."

Sergei also rose and took a long breath. Zinovey Borisych lay dead-strangled-and with a cut on his temple. Under his head on the left side was a little pool of blood, which, however, now flowed no longer from the small wound that had become clotted and congealed with hair.

Sergei carried Zinovey Borisych into the cellar under the floor of the little stone store-room, where he himself had so recently been locked up by the late Boris Timofeich, and then returned to the attic. During this time Katerina Lvovna, with the sleeves of her loose jacket tucked up, and her skirts well lifted, had carefully washed away with bast and soap the blood stain left by Zinovey Borisych on the floor of his bedroom. The water had as yet not cooled in the samovar, out of which Zinovey Borisych, then master of the house, had been comforting his soul with poisoned tea, so the spot could be washed away without leaving any traces.

Katerina Lvovna took a brass slop-basin, and a piece of soaped bast.

"Now give me a light," she said to Sergei, going towards the door. "Lower, throw the light lower," said she, carefully examining all the floors over which Sergei had dragged Zinovey Borisych on the way to the cellar.

Only in two places on the painted floors there were two tiny spots the size of a cherry. Katerina Lvovna rubbed them with the bast and they disappeared.

"That will teach you not to steal on your wife like a thief and watch her," said Katerina Lvovna straightening herself and looking towards the store-house.

"Now it's all over," said Sergei and shuddered at the sound of his own voice.

When they returned to the bedroom a thin red streak of dawn appeared in the eastern sky, and the apple trees, faintly tinted with gold, looked through the green fence of the garden into Katerina Lvovna's room.

The old clerk, with a short fur coat thrown over his shoulders, yawning and crossing himself, crept across the yard from the barn to the kitchen.

Katerina Lvovna pulled the shutters carefully up by their strings, and attentively looked at Sergie as if she wanted to read his soul.

"Well, now you are a merchant," said she placing her white hands on Sergei's shoulders.

Sergei did not answer her.

Sergei's lips trembled and he shook all over as if with ague. Only Katerina Lvovna's lips were cold.

After two days large blisters caused by the use of a heavy spade and crow-bar appeared on Sergei's hands; but, because of them, Zinovey Borisych was so well stowed away in his cellar, that without the aid of his widow or her lover nobody could have found him till the day of the Last Judgment.

Sergei went about with a crimson handkerchief round his neck, and complained that something was sticking in his throat. Even before the marks left on Sergei's throat by Zinovey Borisych's teeth had healed, people began to wonder about Katerina Lvovna's husband. Sergei himself began to talk about him oftener than anyone else. Of an evening he would come and sit down on the bench near the gate with the other young fellows and begin; "It is strange, comrades, that the master has not returned yet."

The other young fellows were also surprised.

Then the news was brought from the mill that the master had hired horses, and had long ago started for home. The postilion who had driven him related that Zinovey Borisych had appeared to be put out, and had dismissed him in a strange manner; about three *versts* from the town near the monastery he had got out of the cart, taken his bag, and walked away. Hearing this strange story people began to wonder still more.

Zinovey Borisych was lost, that was all.

Search was made for him, but nothing could be discovered; it was as if the merchant had vanished off the face of the earth. By the evidence of the postilion, who had been arrested, it was only known that he had left the cart near the river which passed by the monastery. The matter was not cleared up, and in the meantime Katerina Lvovna in her widowed state was able to live more freely with Sergei. They invented stories that Zinovey Borisych had been seen first in one place then in another, but Zinovey Borisych still did not come back and Katerina Lvovna knew better than anyone that it was quite impossible for him to return.

In this way one month passed and another and a third and Katerina Lvovna felt herself with child.

"The capital will be ours, Serezhechka. I shall have an heir," she said to Sergei, and went to the town council to tell them that she was pregnant; to complain that a stoppage in the business had occurred and to ask to be allowed to carry it on.

Why should a commercial undertaking be ruined? Katerina Lvovna was the lawful wife of her husband, there were apparently no debts, so that she ought to be allowed to carry it on. And she was allowed.

Katerina Lvovna lived and reigned and by her orders Sergei was addressed as Sergei Filipych. Then suddenly quite unexpectedly there was a new disaster. A letter came from Liven to the mayor of the town, informing him that Boris Timofeich had traded not only with his own money, but that a great part of the capital in the business belonged to his nephew Fedor Zakharov Lyamin, a minor, and that the business must be looked into and not left entirely in Katerina Lvovna's hands. When this news arrived the mayor spoke about it to Katerina Lvovna, and suddenly a week later-behold an old woman and a small boy arrived from Liven.

"I am the late Boris Timofeich's cousin," said she, "and this is my nephew, Fedor Lyamin." Katerina Lvovna received them.

Sergei, who watched this arrival from the yard and the reception Katerina Lvovna gave them, became as white as an altar-cloth.

"What is the matter with you?" asked the mistress noticing his deadly pallor, as he followed the visitors and remained in the passage watching them.

"Nothing," answered the clerk turning round and going from the passage into the entrance. "I was thinking what a surprise these people from Liven are," he said with a sigh as he closed the door of the entrance after him.

"Well, how will it be now?" Sergei asked Katerina Lvovna as they sat together that night drinking tea. "Now, Katerina Lvovna, all our affairs will turn to ashes."

"Why to ashes, Serezha?"

"Because it will all be divided now. What use will it be to carry on a trifling business?"

"What, Serezha, will it be too little for you?"

"No, it's not about myself I'm thinking. I'm just wondering if we shall have the same happiness."

"How so? Why should we not have happiness, Serezha?"

"Because I love you so much that I want, Katerina Lvovna, to see you a real lady, and not as you have lived so far," answered Sergei Filipich, "and now it will be just the contrary; with the decrease of the capital we will have to sink even lower than before."

"What do I care, Serezha?"

"It may be true, Katerina Lvovna, that perhaps for you it has no interest, but for me, because I respect you, and also to the eyes of the world, mean and envious though they are, it will be terribly painful. You can feel, of course, as you like, but I in my judgment can see that, under these circumstances, I can never be happy."

Sergei began to play upon Katerina Lvovna to this tune; that through Fedia Lyamin he had become the most unhappy man, being deprived in future of the power to exalt and distinguish her, Katerina Lvovna, in the eyes of all the merchants. Every time Sergei brought it to the same conclusion: that if this Fedia did not exist and she gave birth to a child, before the end of nine months after the disappearance of her husband, the whole property would belong to her and that then there would be no end to their happiness.

X

Then Sergei suddenly stopped talking about the heir. As soon as Sergei ceased talking about him, Katerina Lvovna could not get Fedia Lyamin out of her mind or her heart. She became pensive and even less loving to Sergei. When she was asleep, when she was looking after the business, or when she was praying to God, she had but one thought in her mind: "Why is it so? Why indeed should I lose the capital through him? I have suffered so much, I have taken so much sin on my soul," thought Katerina Lvovna, "and he comes here without any trouble and takes it away from me. If at least he were a man, but this child-this boy . . . ."

The early frosts were setting in. Of course no news of Zinovey Borisych came from anywhere. Katerina Lvovna became bigger and went about always more pensive. In the town there was much gossip about her. They wondered why the young Izmaylova, who had so far been barren, and had always grown thin and pined away, now suddenly began to grow larger. All this time the boyish heir Fedia Lyamin wandered about the yard in his light, white squirrel fur coat, and broke the cat-ice on the puddles.

"What are you doing there, Fedor Ignatich?" cried the cook Aksinia to him, as she ran across the yard. "Is it fit for you, a merchant's son, to poke about in the puddles?"

But the heir, who was such a trouble to Katerina Lvovna and to the object of her affections, only frolicked about light-heartedly like a young kid, or slept tranquilly opposite his fond great-aunt, not thinking or realizing that he stood in anybody's way or had diminished anybody's happiness.

At last Fedia caught the chicken-pox, and besides had a bad cold and pain in the chest, so the boy was put to bed. At first he was treated with herbs and simples, but at last a doctor had to be sent for.

The doctor came frequently and prescribed medicines, which were to be given to him at certain hours by his grand-aunt; or sometimes she asked Katerina Lvovna to do it.

"Please, Katerinushka," she would say, "you yourself will soon be a mother, you are awaiting the will of God, be so good . . . ."

Katerina Lvovna never refused the old woman. Whenever she went to the evening service to pray for "the lad Fedor lying on the bed of sickness," or whenever she went to the early liturgy to get him consecrated bread, Katerina Lvovna would sit by the invalid, give him cooling drinks and administer his medicine at the proper time.

So the old woman went to the evening service and to vespers on the eve of the Presentation of the Blessed Virgin, and begged Katerinushka to look after Fedyushka. At that time the boy was already recovering.

Katerina Lvovna came into Fedia's room. He was sitting up in bed in his squirrel coat, reading the "Lives of the Fathers."

"What are you reading, Fedia?" Katerina Lvovna asked, as she sat down in an arm chair.

"I'm reading the 'Lives,' auntie."

"Are they interesting?"

"Very interesting, auntie."

Katerina Lvovna leaned on her hand and watched Fedia's moving lips, when suddenly she was seized, as by demons escaped from their chains, by her former thoughts of all the evil that this boy had caused her, and what a good thing it would be if he were not there.

"Well, what then?" thought Katerina Lvovna, "he is ill, he has to take medicine . . . all sorts of things can happen during illness. . . . One has but to say that the doctor made a mistake with the medicine."

"It's time for your medicine, Fedia."

"Perhaps, auntie," answered the boy, and emptying the spoon he added, "Auntie, these stories of the saints are very interesting."

"Well, go on reading," Katerina Lvovna continued and casting her eyes round the room with a cold glance, let them rest on the frost-covered windows.

"I must order the shutters to be closed," said she going into the sitting-room, and thence into the hall, and then upstairs into her own room where she sat down.

Five minutes later Sergei, in a Romanov short fur coat trimmed with thick seal skin, joined her there.

"Have they closed the shutters?" Katerina Lvovna asked him.

"They have closed them," answered Sergei, snuffing the candles with the snuffers, and stopped near the stove.

They were both silent.

"Vespers will not be finished soon to-day?" asked Katrina Lvovna.

"To-morrow is a big festival; the service will be long," answered Sergei.

There was again silence.

"I'd better go to Fedia; he is alone," said Katerina Lvovna, rising.

"Alone?" asked Sergei, looking at her askance.

"Alone," she answered in a whisper, "what then?"

Their eyes seemed to flash lightning glances to each other, but neither said a word.

Katerina Lvovna went down, and passed through the empty rooms; it was quiet everywhere; the lamps glimmered quietly before the icons; only her own shadow ran along the walls; the closed shutters had made the windows thaw, and the water was dripping from them. Fedia was sitting reading. When he saw Katerina Lvovna he only said:

"Auntie, put this book away, please, and give me that other one from the icon shelf."

Katerina Lvovna did what her nephew asked, and gave him the other book.

"Fedia, don't you want to go to sleep?"

"No, auntie, I want to wait for Granny."

"Why should you wait for her?"

"She promised to bring me a consecrated loaf from Vespers."

Katerina Lvovna suddenly became pale; her own child had moved under her heart, for the first time and a cold feeling passed over her breast. She stood for a time in the middle of the room, and then went out rubbing her cold hands.

"Well," she whispered, quietly entering her bedroom, where she found Sergei still in the same position near the stove.

"What?" asked Sergei scarcely audibly, as if choking.

"He's alone!"

Sergei frowned and began to breathe heavily.

"Come," said Katerina Lvovna, suddenly turning to the door.

Sergei hastily took off his boots and asked:

"What shall we take?"

"Nothing," answered Katerina Lvovna under her breath, and quietly taking him by the hand she drew him after her.

The sick boy shuddered and dropped the book on his knees, when Katerina Lvovna entered his room for the third time.

"What is it, Fedia?"

"Oh, auntie, something frightened me," answered he, with a troubled smile, and cowered into a corner of the bed.

"What frightened you?"

"Who came with you, auntie?"

"Where? Nobody came with me, darling."

"Nobody?"

The boy stretched himself towards the foot of the bed, and screwing up his eyes looked towards the door through which his aunt had entered, and seemed to be re-assured.

"I must have imagined it," said he.

Katerina Lvovna stopped and leaned against the head of her nephew's bed.

Fedia looked up at his aunt, and remarked to her that she had for some reason grown quite pale.

In answer to this observation, Katerina Lvovna only pretended to cough, and looked expectantly at the sitting-room door. But only the floor creaked slightly there.

"I am reading the life of my guardian angel, Saint Theodor Stratelates, auntie. How well he served God."

Katerina Lvovna stood there silent.

"Auntie, won't you sit down and let me read it to you again," said her nephew coaxingly.

"Wait a moment-directly. I must just trim the icon lamp in the drawing-room," answered Katerina Lvovna, and left the room with hasty steps.

In the drawing-room the very faintest whispers could be heard, but, in the general silence, they reached the sharp ears of the child.

"Auntie, what is this? With whom are you whispering there?" cried the boy, with tears in his voice. "Come here, auntie, I am afraid," he cried again a second later, even more tearfully and he heard Katerina Lvovna say in the drawing-room "Well!" which he thought was addressed to him.

"What are you afraid of?" asked Katerina Lvovna, in a somewhat hoarse voice, as she came into the room with a firm, decided step, and stopped before his bed in such a position that the door to the drawing-room was hidden from the invalid by her body. Then she said, "Lie down!"

"I don't want to, auntie."

"No, Fedia, listen to me and lie down; it is time to lie down," Katerina Lvovna repeated.

"Why, auntie? I don't at all want to."

"No, you must lie down; lie down at once," said Katerina Lvovna, in a changed shaky voice and seizing the boy under the arms, she put his head on the pillow.

At that moment Fedia shrieked with fear; he had perceived Sergei pale and barefooted entering the room.

Katerina Lvovna placed the palm of her hand over the frightened child's open mouth and cried:

"Quickly now; hold him tight; keep him from struggling."

Sergei seized Fedia by the arms and legs, and Katerina Lvovna with one rapid movement covered the childish face of the victim with a large down pillow and threw herself on it with her firm elastic bosom.

For four minutes there was the silence of the grave in the room.

"He's dead," whispered Katerina Lvovna, and had only just risen to put everything in order again, when the walls of the quiet house, that had concealed so many crimes, were shaken by deafening blows: the windows rattled, the floors shook, the chairs of the hanging icon lamps trembled and fantastic shadows flitted around the walls.

Sergei shuddered and ran off as fast as his legs would carry him. Katerina Lvovna followed him, and the noise and hubbub pursued them. It seemed as if some unearthly power was shaking the guilty house to its foundations.

Katerina Lvovna was afraid that Sergei, in his fear, would run into the yard and betray himself but he rushed straight to the attic.

In the darkness at the top of the stairs Sergei struck his forehead against the half-opened door and with a groan fell down, completely losing his senses from superstitious fear.

"Zinovey Borisych, Zinovey Borisych," he mumbled as he fell down the stairs head foremost, knocking Katerina Lvovna off her feet and carrying her with him in his fall.

"Where?" asked she.

"There, above us; he flew past with a sheet of iron. There, there again. Oh, oh!" cried Sergei, "it thunders, it thunders again."

It was quite plain now that in the street numberless hands were knocking at all the windows, and someone was trying to break in the door.

"You fool-get up, you fool," cried Katerina Lvovna, and with these words she hastened to Fedia, settled his dead head on the pillow in the most natural sleeping position, and with a firm hand opened the door, through which a crowd of people streamed into the house.

It was a terrible sight. Katerina Lvovna, looking out over the heads of the crowd that was besieging the porch, saw streams of strange people climbing over the high wooden fence into the yard, and heard the moaning of many human voices in the street.

Before Katerina Lvovna was able to understand anything, she was crushed back into the room by the crowd that surrounded the porch.

All this alarm had been caused in this way.

At Vespers on the eve of one of the twelve great festivals, there are always immense crowds in the churches of the provincial but important industrial town in which Katerina Lvovna lived, and in the church that was celebrating its special festival such numbers of people would collect that not even an apple could have fallen to the ground. It was the custom for choirs, composed of young men belonging to the merchant classes, led by a special precentor, also a lover of the vocal art, to sing in the church on such occasions.

Our people are godly, assiduous churchgoers, and artistic as well. Ecclesiastical magnificence and harmonious singing constitute one of their chief and purest enjoyments. Wherever the choirs sing, nearly half the town assembles to hear them, especially the youth of the merchant classes: the clerks, the boys, the youths, the hands from the factories and workshops, and even the manufacturers themselves with their better halves; all crowd together in the same church; everybody wants to be there if only in the porch, or under the windows, despite burning heat or hard frost, to hear how the octaves swell, or the powerful tenor executes the most difficult variations.

The parish church of the Izmailov family was consecrated in honour of the Presentation in the Temple of the Blessed Virgin, and therefore on the eve of that festival, at the time that the events just related occurred, the youth of the whole town was collected there, and they left the church in a noisy crowd talking about the merits of a well-known tenor, and the accidental blunders of a no less celebrated bass.

Not all were occupied with these musical questions; there were some people in the crowd who interested themselves in other subjects.

"Yes, boys, fine things are related about that young Izmailova," said a young mechanic, who had been brought from Petersburg by one of the merchants for his steam factory, "they say," continued he, "that she and their young clerk Sergei are making love every minute."

"Everybody knows that," answered a man in a sheepskin coat covered with blue cloth. "She was not in church this evening either."

"Church indeed? That wicked young woman is so odious, that she no longer fears God, nor her conscience, nor the eye of man."

"See they have a light," remarked the mechanic pointing to a bright stripe between the shutters.

"Look through the chink-see what they are doing," called several voices.

The mechanic climbed on to the shoulders of two of his companions, and had scarcely put his eye to the opening in the shutter when he shouted at the top of his voice.

"Good people, brothers, they are smothering somebody here, smothering somebody."

And the mechanic began desperately to knock at the shutters, a dozen others followed his example, and springing to the windows began hammering at them with their fists.

The crowd increased in numbers every minute, and the Izmaylov's house was beseiged as has been related.

"I myself saw it, I saw it with my own eyes," the mechanic affirmed pointing to the dead body of Fedia. "The boy was lying on his bed and they were both suffocating him."

Sergei was taken to the police station that same evening; Katerina Lvovna was led to her upper room and two guards were stationed over her.

It was unbearably cold in the Ismaylov's house, the stoves were unheated; the door did not remain closed for an instant; great crowds of curious people followed on each other's heels. All came to look at Fedia lying in his coffin and at another large coffin quite covered up to the lid with a wide shroud. On Fedia's forehead was a white satin band which covered the red line that was left after the skull had been opened. The post-mortem examination proved that Fedia's death had been caused by suffocation, and Sergei, when he was confronted with the corpse, began to cry at the first words of the priest who told him of the Last Judgment and of the punishment of the unrepentant, and candidly confessed not only the murder of Fedia, but also begged that Zinovey Borisych, who had been buried by him without a funeral service, should be disinterred. The corpse of Katerina Lvovna's husband, that had been buried in dry sand, was as yet not entirely decomposed. It was taken out and laid in a large coffin. To the general horror Sergei said that his accomplice in both these cruel murders had been the young mistress. To all the questions put to her Katerina Lvovna only answered: "I know nothing about this. I know nothing about it." They obliged Sergei to give evidence before her. Having heard his confession, Katerina Lvovna looked at him with dumb astonishment but without anger, and then said unconcernedly:

"Since he wished to tell it, I have nothing to disavow. I killed them."

"Why did you do it?" she was asked.

"For him," she answered pointing to Sergei, who hung his head.

The criminals were taken to prison, and this terrible case, which had attracted general attention and indignation, soon came up for judgment. At the end of February Sergei and the widow of the third guild merchant, Katerina Lvovna, were condemned to be flogged on the market-place of their town, and then to be sent to penal servitude. In the beginning of March, on a cold frosty morning the executioner inflicted the appointed number of blue-red lashes on Katerina Lvovna's bare, white back and then also administered the allotted portion of strokes on Sergei's shoulders, and branded his handsome face with the three marks of a convict.

During the whole of this time, for some reason, Sergei aroused much more sympathy than Katerina Lvovna. Dirty and bloodstained he stumbled when he descended from the black scaffold, but Katerina Lvovna came down quietly, only taking care that the thick shift and coarse convict jacket should not come in contact with her lacerated back. Even in the prison hospital, when they handed her child to her she only said: "What do I want with him!" turned to the wall and without a groan, without a complaint, fell with her bosom on the hard pallet.

THE gang of convicts with which Sergei and Katerina Lvovna went started when the spring, according to the calendar, had begun, but the sun, as the popular saying is, "shone brightly but did not warm."

Katerina Lvovna's child was given to Boris Timofeich's old cousin to be brought up, as the infant being considered the legitimate son of the criminal's husband remained the sole heir to the whole of the Izmaylov's property. Katrina Lvovna was very pleased at this, and gave up her baby with great indifference. Her love for the father, as is the case with many passionate women, was not transferred in the slightest degree to the child.

Besides for her neither light nor darkness existed, neither goodness nor badness, neither sorrow nor joy; she understood nothing, loved nobody, not even herself. She only awaited impatiently the departure of the gang of convicts, as she hoped on the way to see her Serezhenhka again, and she even forgot to think about the child.

Katerina Lvovna's hopes did not deceive her: heavily fettered with chains and branded, Sergei passed through the prison gates with the party in which she was.

Man is able to accommodate himself, as far as possible, to every horrible position in which he may find himself, and in every position he is able to retain the power of pursuing his own scanty pleasures; but Katerina Lvovna had no need to adapt herself to circumstances; she again saw Sergei, and with him even the convict's path was bright with happiness for her.

Katerina Lvovna took but few things of value with her in her linen sack, and even less money. But long before they reached Nizhni she had given all this to the guards who accompanied them, for the permission to walk next to Sergei on the way, or to be allowed to stand with him and embrace him for an hour on dark nights in a corner of the narrow corridor of the cold halting-stations.

But Katerina Lvovna's branded friend became very unaffectionate towards her; every word he said to her was harsh; he did not set much value on the secret meetings with her, for which she went without food and drink and gave away the most precious twenty-five copeck pieces out of her already lean purse, and more than once he said:

"Instead of paying the guard to come and rub against the corners of the corridor with me, you'd do better to give me the money."

"I only gave a quarter, Serezhenka," said Katerina Lvovna in self defence.

"Isn't a quarter money? How many quarters have you picked up on the way? You've distributed many apparently."

"But, Serezha, we have seen each other."

"Well, what good is that? What sort of joy have we in meeting after all this suffering? You ought to curse your life and not think of meetings."

"It's all the same to me, Serezha, if I can only see you."

"That's all nonsense," answered Sergei.

Sometimes Katerina Lvovna bit her lips to blood at such answers, and sometimes in the darkness of their nocturnal meetings tears of anger and vexation rose to her eyes, that had never wept before; but she bore everything; was always silent, and tried to deceive herself.

In this manner, in these new relations to each other, they reached Nizhni Novgorod. There the party was joined by another detachment of convicts, on their way to Siberia from the Moscow district.

In this large gang, among a number of all sorts of people, there were in the women's division two very interesting characters; one was the wife of a soldier, Fiona, from Yaroslavl, a magnificently beautiful woman, tall, with a thick black plait and languid hazel eyes, over which the long lashes hung like a mysterious veil; and the other a pretty girl of seventeen, with a sharp face, delicate skin, a tiny mouth, dimples in her fresh cheeks, and fair golden locks that capriciously peeped out on her forehead from beneath her striped convict kerchief. This girl was called by the others Sonetka.

Fiona, the beauty, had a soft and lazy disposition. In her party all knew her and none of the men were specially delighted to have success with her, and none of them were mortified to see that she allowed the same favours to anybody else who tried for them.

"Aunt Fiona is the kindest of women, she never snubs anyone," all the convicts said jestingly.

But Sonetka was quite of another sort.

They said about her:

"She's like an eel, she twirls round your hands, but you can never get hold of her."

Sonetka had her own taste, made her choice, and perhaps even a very severe choice; she wanted a passion to be presented to her, not as an ordinary dish, but under a highly spiced sauce, with sufferings and sacrifices; but Fiona had the simplicity of the Russian woman, who is even too lazy to say, "go away," to anybody and only knows that she is a woman. Such women are very highly prized in robber bands, gangs of convicts, and in the Petersburg social-democratic communes.

The appearance of these two women in the party which was now united with the gang in which Sergei and Katerina Lvovna were, had a very tragic result for the latter.

XIV

In the first day's march of the two united detachments from Nizhni to Kasan, Sergei began, in a very marked manner, to try to ingratiate himself into the favour of the soldier's wife Fiona, and not without success. The languid beauty Fiona did not cause Sergei to want her long as, owing to her goodness, she never allowed anyone to pine for her. At the third or fourth station Katerina Lvovna had, by means of bribery, arranged a meeting with Sergei, and lay awake expecting the guard on duty to come up to her, nudge her and whisper quietly: "Run quickly." The door opened once and some woman ran into the corridor; the door opened again and another convict jumped quickly from her pallet, and disappeared after the guard; at last somebody pulled the jacket with which Katerina Lvovna was covered. The young woman sprang hurriedly from the boards, that many convicts had polished so well with their sides, threw her jacket over her shoulders, and nudged the guard who was standing near her.

When Katerina Lvovna went along the dark corridor, which was lighted only in one place by a tallow dip, she knocked up against two or three couples who could not be seen at a distance, and in passing the door of the men's ward, she heard suppressed laughter that came through the little window cut in it.

"Eh, they're having fun," the guard who conducted Katerina Lvovna mumbled discontentedly, and taking her by the shoulders he pushed her into a corner and went away.

Katerina Lvovna groping about felt a woman's jacket and a beard; her other hand touched a woman's hot face.

"Who's that?" Sergei asked in an undertone.

"What are you doing here? Who are you with?"

Katerina Lvovna tore her rival's handkerchief off. The latter ran away, and tripping over some one fell down.

Hearty laughter resounded from the men's ward.

"Villain," hissed Katerina Lvovna and hit Sergei across the face with the end of the handkerchief she had torn from his new friend's head.

Sergei lifted his hand, but Katerina Lvovna slipped quickly away along the corridor, and regained her door. The laughter in the men's ward became so loud that the sentry, who was standing apathetically near the dip, spitting at the toes of his boots, lifted his head and growled:

"Hsss!"

Katerina Lvovna lay down in silence, and remained thus till morning. She wanted to say to herself: "I don't love him," and felt that she loved him more passionately than ever, and before her eyes she saw the whole time, how he lay there with one trembling hand under the other woman's head and with the other embracing her hot shoulders.

The poor woman wept and prayed against her wish that, the hand might be at that moment under her head, and that the other arm might be embracing her own hysterically shaking shoulders.

"Well, in any case, give me my handkerchief," said the soldier's wife Fiona, the next morning arousing her.

"So it was you!"

"Give it me, please."

"Why do you part us?"

"How do I part you? As if this is love or interest? Why do you get cross?"

Katerina Lvovna thought for a moment, and then taking the torn handkerchief from under her pillow she threw it at Fiona, and turned to the wall.

She felt better.

"Faugh!" she said to herself. "Is it possible that I am jealous of this painted wash-tub? The devil take her! To compare myself with her makes me sick."

"Look here, Katerina Lvovna, just listen to me," said Sergi the next day on the road. "First understand, I beg you, that I am not your Zinovey Borisych, and secondly that you are no longer the great merchant's wife. So don't blaze up. These grand airs are no good now."

Katerina Lvovna did not answer, and for a week she went along without exchanging a word or a look with Sergei. As the injured party she showed character, and did not want to make the first step towards reconciliation in this, her first quarrel, with Sergei.

In the meantime while Katerina Lvovna was cross with Sergei he began to talk nonsense and joke with fair little Sonetka. Sometimes he would bow to her and say: "Our charmer," or he would smile, or find an opportunity of meeting her, of embracing and pressing her to himself. Katerina Lvovna saw all this and her heart only boiled the more.

"Should I get reconciled to him?" Katerina Lvovna thought as she staggered along, not seeing the ground under her feet.

But now, more than ever, her pride would not allow her to take the first step towards reconciliation. During this time Sergei became more and more intimate with Sonetka, and all began to whisper that the unapproachable Sonetka, who like an eel twirled round everybody's hands without being caught, had somehow become much more tame.

"Do you see that," said Fiona to Katerina Lvovna, "you cried about me. Now what have I done to you? I had my chance, but it's over. You'd better look to Sonetka."

"All my pride has deserted me, I must certainly be reconciled now," Katerina Lvovna decided, only thinking what would be the best way to set about the reconciliation.

Sergei himself helped her out of this difficult position.

"Lvovna," he called to her during the rest, "come to me for a minute this night; I have some business for you."

Katerina Lvovna was silent.

"What, are you still cross? Won't you come?"

Katerina Lvovna again made no answer.

However, Sergei and all the others who watched Katerina Lvovna saw that when they were approaching the halting-place she kept getting nearer to the guard, and shoved into his hand seventeen copecks, some alms she had received from the communes.

"As soon as I collect them I will give you ten copecks more," begged Katerina Lvovna.

The guard hid the money in his cuff and said:

"All right."

When these discussions were over Sergei grunted and winked at Sonetka.

"Ah, my Katerina Lvovna," said he, embracing her as he mounted the steps of the halting-station, "there's no woman like her in the whole world, comrades."

"Katerina Lvovna blushed and became breathless with happiness.

At night, as soon as the door opened quietly, she jumped up; trembling she groped for Sergei with her hands in the dark corridor.

"My Katia," whispered Sergei embracing her.

"Oh, my own rascal," answered Katerina Lvovna through her tears, pressing her lips to his.

The guard walked about the corridor stopping to spit on his boots and went on again, the tired convicts snored on the other side of the doors, a mouse gnawed a feather under the stove, the crickets vied with each other in their loud chirps, and Katerina Lvovna still enjoyed her bliss.

But ecstasies tire and the inevitable prose has its turn.

"I'm in deadly pain. Right from the ankle to the knee it gnaws my bones," complained Sergei sitting with Katerina Lvovna on the floor in the corner of the corridor.

"What's to be done, Serezhenka?" she asked, nestling under the skirts of his coat.

"All that remains to be done, is to ask to be put into hospital in Kasan."

"Oh! What do you mean, Serezha?"

"What can I do? This pain will be my death."

"How can you remain when I shall be driven on?"

"What's to be done? It rubs, I tell you it rubs; the chain is eating into the bone. If I had woollen stockings to put on that might help," said Sergei a minute later.

"Stockings? I still have some. New stockings, Sergei."

"What of that?" answered Sergei.

Without saying another word, Katerina Lvovna quickly vanished into the ward, rummaged in her bag on the boards and then hastily returned to Sergei with a pair of thick blue woollen stockings with bright red clocks at the sides.

"Now it will be all right," said Sergei, taking leave of Katerina Lvovna and accepting her last stockings.

Katerina Lvovna returned to her boards quite happy and was soon sound asleep.

When she had returned to the corridor she had not noticed that Sonetka went out of the ward, nor had she heard her return just before morning.

All this took place only two days' march from Kasan.

A cold rainy day, with gusts of wind and sleet, inhospitably greeted the party of convicts when they left the stuffy halting-station. Katerina Lvovna came out fairly cheerfully, but she had hardly taken her place in the row when she turned green and trembled all over. It grew black before her eyes, and all her joints ached and weakened. Sonetka stood before her in the well-known pair of blue woollen stockings with red clocks.

Katerina Lvovna started on her way almost lifeless; only her eyes were fixed with a terrible look on Sergei, and she never took them off him.

At the first halt she quietly went up to Sergei, whispered "Scoundrel," and quite unexpectedly spat in his face.

Sergei wanted to fall upon her, but the others held him back.

"Just you wait," said he wiping himself.

"All the same she treats you audaciously," jeered the other convicts, and Sonetka greeted him with specially gay laughter.

This intrigue into which Sonetka had entered was quite to her taste.

"This is not the last you will hear of it," Sergei threatened Katerina Lvovna.

Worn out by the long distance and the bad weather, Katerina Lvovna with a broken heart slept restlessly on the hard boards at night in the halting-station and did not hear two men come into the women's ward.

When they entered Sonetka sat up on her pallet and silently pointed to Katerina Lvovna, lay down again, and covered herself up with her coat.

At that moment Katerina Lvovna's coat was thrown over her head, and the thick end of a double-twisted cord was swung with all the strength of a peasant's arm across her back, which was only covered by a coarse shift.

Katerina Lvovna shrieked but her voice could not be heard under the coat in which her head was wrapt up. She struggled, but also without success, as a burly convict was sitting on her shoulders holding her arms.

"Fifty," counted a voice at last, and it was not difficult to recognize the voice of Sergei, and then the nocturnal visitors disappeared behind the door.

Katerina Lvovna disentangled her head and got up, but nobody was there, only not far off somebody under a coat tittered malevolently. Katerina Lvovna recognized Sonetka's laugh.

This insult passed all measure, and there was also no limit to the feeling of wrath which boiled up at that moment in Katerina Lvovna's soul. Not knowing what she did she rushed forward and fell unconscious on Fiona's breast and was caught in her arms.

On that full bosom, which so lately had diverted with its sweet depravity Katerina Lvovna's faithless lover, she now sobbed out her own unbearable sorrow, and pressed herself close to her stupid and coarse rival, as a child would to its mother. They were now equal. They were both of equal price and both cast away.

They were equal! —the caprice of a passing moment-Fiona; and she who had committed that drama of love, Katerina Lvovna.

Nothing was an insult to Katerina Lvovna now. Having shed her tears she became hardened and with wooden calmness prepared to go out to the roll-call.

The drum sounded Rapa-ta-tap. The prisoners went out into the yard; the chained and the unchained Sergei and Fiona, Sonetka and Katerina Lvovna; the schismatic fettered to the Jew, the Pole on the same chain with the Tarter.

All crowded together, then formed into some sort of order and started.

It was a most desolate picture: a small number of people torn from the light and deprived of every shadow of hope of a better future-sinking into the cold black mud of the common road. Everything around was frightfully ugly: unending mud, a grey sky, the leafless wet cytisus and the ravens with bristling feathers sitting in their spreading branches. The wind sighed and raged, howled and tore.

In these hellish, soul-rending sounds that completed the horror of the picture there seemed to echo the advice of the wife of the biblical Job: "Curse the day of your birth and die."

Those who do not wish to listen to these words; those who are not attracted by the thoughts of death even in this sorrowful position, but are frightened by them, must try to silence these warring voices by something even more monstrous. The simple man understands this very well; he lets lose all his animal simplicity, begins to play the fool, to laugh at himself, at other people and at feelings. At no time very delicate he becomes doubly bad.

* * * * *

"Well, my merchant's wife, is your honour in good health?" Sergei asked Katerina Lvovna impudently as soon as the village where they had passed the night, disappeared out of sight behind the wet hills.

With these words he turned at once to Sonetka, covered her up with his coat, and began to sing in a high falsetto voice:

> "In the shade behind the window a fair head appears;
> You don't sleep, my tormenter, you don't sleep, you rogue.
> With my coat skirt I shall cover you, so that none shall see."

When he sang these words Sergei put his arms round Sonetka and gave her a loud kiss before the whole party.

Katerina Lvovna saw all this, and yet did not see it. She went along like a lifeless person. The others nudged her and pointed out how Sergei was playing the fool with Sonetka. She had become an object of ridicule.

"Leave her alone," Fiona said, trying to defend her, when one of the party attempted to laugh at Katerina Lvovna as she stumbled blindly along; "you devils, don't you see that the woman is quite ill?"

"Probably she got wet feet," a young convict said waggishly.

"Naturally, she's from a merchant's race; had a delicate up-bringing," answered Sergei.

"Of course, if she had warm stockings, it would not be so bad," continued he.

Katerina Lvovna seemed to wake up.

"Vile serpent," she uttered, unable to bear it any more; "laugh at me, villain, laugh at me."

"No, I am not laughing at all, my merchant's wife. I only say it because Sonetka wants to sell some stockings that are still quite good, so I thought our merchant's wife might perhaps buy them."

Many laughed; Katerina Lvovna walked on like an automaton.

The weather became worse. From the dark clouds that covered the sky wet snow fell in large flakes, that melted as soon as it reached the ground, and added to the impassable mud. At last a long leaden line could be seen; the other side of it could not be distinguished. This line was the Volga. Over the Volga a strong wind blew, and rocked the slowly-rising, dark-crested waves backwards and forwards.

The gang of convicts, wet through and shivering, came slowly up to the river's bank and stopped to wait for the ferry-boat.

The dark wet ferry-boat arrived; the guards began to find places for the convicts.

"They say there is vodka to be had on this ferry-boat," observed one of the convicts, when the ferry-boat, covered with large flakes of wet snow, had put off from the bank and was rocking on the waves of the rough river.

"Yes, it would be a good thing to have a drop now," said Sergei, and persecuting Katerina Lvovna for Sonetka's amusement, he continued: "Well now, merchant's wife, for old friendship's sake treat us to some vodka. Don't be stingy. Remember, my ungracious one, our former love, how you and I, my joy, loved each other, how we passed long autumn nights together, and sent your relations in secret, without priest or deacon, to their eternal rest."

Katerina Lvovna was shivering with cold. Besides the cold that pierced through her wet clothes to the very bones, something more was going on in Katerina Lvovna. Her head was burning like fire; the dilated pupils of her eyes shone brightly, her eyes wandered wildly round, or looking before her, rested immovable on the rolling waves.

"Yes, I would gladly drink some vodka. I can bear it no longer," Sonetka chimed in.

"Merchant's wife, won't you stand us a drink?" Sergei continued to annoy her.

"Where's your conscience?" said Fiona, shaking her head reproachfully.

"It's no honour to yourself to have such a conscience," said the convict Gorushek in support of the soldier's wife.

"If you're not ashamed before her, ye might be ashamed for her, before others."

"Get along, you worldly old snuff-box," shouted Sergei at Fiona. "Ashamed indeed! What have I to be ashamed of! Perhaps I never loved her. . . . and now Sonetka's worn-out boot is worth more to me than her phiz-the draggle-tailed cat! What can you canswer to that? Let her love crooked-mouthed Gorushek or else" —he looked round at the guard who was sitting on his horse wrapped up in his burka and military cap with its cocade, and added —"better still, let her make up to the guard. Under his burka she would at least not get wet when it rains."

"And all would call her the officer's lady," tittered Sonetka.

"Of course it would be a trifle then to get stockings," continued Sergei.

Katerina Lvovna did not defend herself: she only looked more fixedly at the waves and her lips moved. Between Sergei's base talk she heard the roar and sighing of the rising and breaking waves. Suddenly out of one broken billow she saw the blue head of Boris Timofeich appear, from another her husband looked out, and rolled about embracing Fedia's drooping head. Katerina Lvovna tried to remember a prayer and moved her lips, but her lips only whispered: "How you and I loved each other; sat long autumn nights together; sent people from the light of day by violent deaths."

Katerina Lvovna shuddered. Her wandering gaze became fixed and grew wild. Once or twice her arms stretched out into space aimlessly, and then fell down again. Another minute-she rocked about, not taking her eyes off the dark waves, bent forwards, seized Sonetka by the legs and with one bound threw herself and her overboard.

All were petrified with amazement.

Katerina Lvovna appeared on the top of a wave, and again dived under; another wave brought Sonetka in view.

"A boat-hook, throw them a boat-hook!" they shouted on the ferry.

A heavy boat-hook attached to a long rope was thrown over-board and fell into the water. Sonetka again was lost to sight. In two seconds the rapid current carried her away from the ferry and she again raised her arms, but at the same moment Katerina Lvovna rose from another wave, almost to the waist above the water, and threw herself on Sonetka like a strong pike on a soft-finned minnow, and neither appeared again.

www.ingramcontent.com/pod-product-compliance
Lightning Source LLC
LaVergne TN
LVHW021711210726
843510LV00015B/1396